Dear Parent:

Congratulations! Your child is taking the first steps on an exciting journey. The destination? Independent reading!

STEP INTO READING® will help your child get there. The program offers books at five levels that accompany children from their first attempts at reading to reading success. Each step includes fun stories, fiction and nonfiction, and colorful art. There are also Step into Reading Sticker Books, Step into Reading Math Readers, and Step into Reading Phonics Readers— a complete literacy program with something to interest every child.

Learning to Read, Step by Step!

Ready to Read Preschool–Kindergarten
• big type and easy words • rhyme and rhythm • picture clues
For children who know the alphabet and are eager to begin reading.

Reading with Help Preschool–Grade 1
• basic vocabulary • short sentences • simple stories
For children who recognize familiar words and sound out new words with help.

Reading on Your Own Grades 1–3
• engaging characters • easy-to-follow plots • popular topics
For children who are ready to read on their own.

Reading Paragraphs Grades 2–3
• challenging vocabulary • short paragraphs • exciting stories
For newly independent readers who read simple sentences with confidence.

Ready for Chapters Grades 2–4
• chapters • longer paragraphs • full-color art
For children who want to take the plunge into chapter books but still like colorful pictures.

STEP INTO READING® is designed to give every child a successful reading experience. The grade levels are only guides. Children can progress through the steps at their own speed, developing confidence in their reading, no matter what their grade.

Remember, a lifetime love of reading starts with a single step!

www.stepintoreading.com

Educators and librarians, for a variety of teaching tools, visit us at
www.randomhouse.com/teachers

Library of Congress Cataloging-in-Publication Data
Scarry, Richard.
The worst helper ever! / by Richard Scarry. — 1st Random House ed.
     p.   cm. — (Step into reading. A step 2 book)
SUMMARY: Farmer Pig needs help on the farm, but that is not what he gets from Charlie Cat.
ISBN 0-307-26100-X (trade) — ISBN 0-375-99990-6 (lib. bdg.)
[1. Animals—Fiction. 2. Farm life—Fiction.]
I. Title.   II. Series: Step into reading. Step 2 book.
PZ7 .S327Wor 2003 [E]—dc21   2002153661

Printed in the United States of America   12 11 10 9 8 7 6 5 4 3
First Random House Edition

STEP INTO READING, RANDOM HOUSE, and the Random House colophon are registered trademarks
of Random House, Inc.

Richard Scarry

The Worst Helper Ever!

Random House 🏠 New York

Wake up, Farmer Pig.

It's time to go to work.

What a busy, busy day!

You need a helper,
Farmer Pig.

Hello, Charlie Cat!
Are you busy?

No, I'm not busy,
Farmer Pig.

Can you help me,
Charlie Cat?

Yes, Farmer Pig.
I can drive your truck.

Oh, dear!
Not THAT way,
Charlie Cat.

Drive OVER the water,
not through it!

Charlie Cat,
you are the
worst helper ever!

But Farmer Fox is
a good helper.

Oh, dear!

Be careful, Charlie Cat.

No more mistakes!

Can you help me
in the barn,
Charlie Cat?

Yes, I can milk the cow,
Farmer Pig.

Oh, dear!

Not THAT way,
Charlie Cat.

Keep the milk IN the pail.
Don't spill it!

Can you help me
in the garden,
Charlie Cat?

Yes, I can water the garden,
Farmer Pig.

Oh, dear!

Not THAT way,
Charlie Cat.

Water the garden,
not the kitchen!

Please sit down,
Charlie Cat.
It's time to eat.

No more mistakes now!

Let me clear the table,
Farmer Pig.

Oh, dear!
Not THAT way,
Charlie Cat.

29

I am taking you back
to town, Charlie Cat.

But this time I'll drive.

We all make mistakes.

Don't we, Farmer Pig?